WALT DISNEY'S 101 Dalmatians

Based on the book "The Hundred and One Dalmatians"
by Dodie Smith

A GOLDEN BOOK · NEW YORK
Western Publishing Company, Inc., Racine, Wisconsin 53404

ISBN: 0-307-02037-1   MCMXCI

"DOGNAPPING! FIFTEEN PUPPIES STOLEN!" said the newspaper headlines.

It was a sad day in the small London house of Roger and Anita Radcliff. Only yesterday they had been the proud owners of seventeen beautiful Dalmatians. Now only two—Pongo and Perdita—remained. And everyone was heartbroken.

"I'm afraid we've done everything possible to find the puppies," said Roger sorrowfully.

"Perdy," said Pongo to the puppies' weeping mother, "our humans are getting nowhere in the search. But I have a plan—the Twilight Bark. It's the fastest way to send news. If the London dogs have seen our puppies, they'll let us know. We'll send word tonight!"

When the Radcliffs took Pongo and Perdita to the park that evening, Pongo barked the alert. He waited for an answer. Then he barked the news of the stolen puppies and asked for help.

Far out in the country, distant barking reached the shaggy ears of Colonel, a retired army dog, and his friend, a cat called Sergeant Tibs.

"Fifteen puppies!" exclaimed Sergeant Tibs. "That's odd. I heard puppies barking down at the old deserted De Vil mansion the other night. Let's go have a look."

The two friends made their way through the snow. They saw smoke coming from the chimney of the old house.

Sergeant Tibs climbed in through a broken window. Inside, he saw an evil-looking woman, two evil-looking men, and—Tibs counted carefully—ninety-nine Dalmatian puppies! Fifteen wore collars and licenses. They were Pongo and Perdita's missing puppies!

The woman, Cruella De Vil, screamed at the two men, "The job must be done tonight!"

"But the pups ain't big enough," answered one of the men. "You couldn't get a dozen fur coats out of the whole kaboodle."

"Oh, my!" thought Sergeant Tibs. "Those pups are going to be made into coats! I've got to tell the Colonel."

He crept silently out to where his friend was waiting.

The Colonel immediately sent a message that the puppies had been found. When the message reached them, Pongo and Perdita leaped out an open window and ran to the rescue.

Meanwhile, Tibs went back inside to help the puppies. He urged them to escape, one by one, through a hole in the door. But the last puppy yelped as he squeezed through, and the evil men came to investigate.

Pongo and Perdita had been
following barked directions all
night. Now, at a crossroads, Pongo
was stopped by the Colonel,
who stood nearby.

"Quick! There's trouble!" he
said, and Pongo and Perdita raced
on toward the mansion.

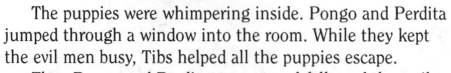

The puppies were whimpering inside. Pongo and Perdita jumped through a window into the room. While they kept the evil men busy, Tibs helped all the puppies escape.

Then Pongo and Perdita ran out and followed the trail to a warm barn. They were soon surrounded by their puppies.

"Are all fifteen of you here?" asked Pongo.

Then he noticed that the barn was filled with dozens of other puppies. "Ninety-nine of you!" gasped Pongo.

"Most of us were bought at pet shops," said one puppy. "That Cruella De Vil wants to make spotted coats out of us."

The Colonel warned the Dalmatians that the evil men were coming toward the barn. All the dogs swarmed out the back door and away.

Mile after mile, the evil men—and Cruella De Vil, in her big car—followed the dogs' trail. The dogs stopped to hide under a bridge.

They heard a distant message being barked to them. The message was from a big black Labrador who had a hiding place for the Dalmatians. He led them to a deserted blacksmith shop in the next village.

Pointing to a van outside the window, the Labrador said, "When its engine is fixed, you can hitch a ride home."

Just then, Cruella De Vil and her helpers pulled up. As Pongo tried to think of ways to escape, two puppies tumbled out of the fireplace. They were covered with coal-black soot.

"Perdita," said Pongo, "I've got an idea. We'll all roll in the soot. We'll all be black Labradors."

The puppies rolled in the soot. Pongo and Perdita joined
them.

"Hurry," urged the Labrador. "The van is almost ready to
leave."

The army of puppies began marching past Cruella De Vil and into the van. She studied them suspiciously.

Then Cruella's eyes widened. As the last puppy headed for the van, a lump of melting snow fell on its head. The soot was washed away—leaving the white coat and black markings of a Dalmatian.

"It can't be!" Cruella screamed. She called her helpers. "The puppies are in that van!"

The van was already moving. With the last puppy in his mouth, Pongo leaped for the tailgate. Perdita pulled him and the puppy to safety.

Cruella wanted to follow the van. She tried to turn her big car around in the narrow village street, but her helpers were blocking the way.

"We made it!" Pongo said happily.

But his happiness was not to last. Although the driver was driving fast, Cruella had caught up. She pulled up alongside the van and tried to force it off the road.

"Crazy driver!" shouted the van driver. "What are you trying to do?"

Cruella continued to push the van to the side of the road. It teetered on the edge of a deep ditch.

Then Pongo and Perdita heard one of Cruella's helpers say, "Watch me shove that van into the ditch."

He drew up alongside the two careening vehicles. But the road was narrow and slippery. At a curve, Cruella's car and her helpers' truck crashed off the road in a tangle of metal.

The van swerved out of the way and then sped on. "Oh, I give up," Cruella sobbed.

Back at the Radcliff house, Roger and Anita were sad, even though it was Christmas Eve. They missed their beloved Dalmatians.

Suddenly, a host of happy, barking black dogs filled the room.

Roger saw something familiar in the shape of a big dog's head. He dusted it off with his handkerchief. "It's Pongo!" he cried, dancing around the room with the dog.

With a pair of feather dusters, Roger and Anita uncovered the familiar spotted coats of their Dalmatians. Pongo, Perdita, and their fifteen puppies were all safe at home.

"But look, Anita," said Roger, "there are more puppies everywhere! There must be a hundred of them. Let's see." And he began to count them.

"One hundred and one Dalmatians," Roger said when he had finished.

"What will we do with all of them?" gasped Anita.

"We'll keep them," Roger answered.

"What?" said Anita. "In this little house?"

Roger picked his way through the puppies to the piano. "We'll buy a big place in the country," he said.

Then Roger began to play and sing.

We'll have a Dalmatian plantation—
A Dalmatian plantation, I say.

A life-long vacation…complete resignation
To sweet relaxation and play.

Our new population is no complication,
We have enough money for remuneration.

We'll have a Dalmatian plantation,
Where our population can roam.

In this location, our whole aggregation
Will love our plantation home.